Northamptonshire County Council
Libraries and Information Service

RYAN, M.

Robbie and the alien

Please return or renew this item by the last date shown.
You may renew items (unless they have been requested
by another customer) by telephoning, writing to or calling
in at any library. 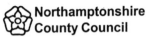 100% recycled paper   *BKS 1 (5/95)*

Text copyright © Margaret Ryan
Illustrations copyright © Bridget MacKeith 1999

First published in Great Britain in 1999
by Macdonald Young Books
This edition published in 2002 by Hodder Wayland,
an imprint of Hodder Children's Books

Hodder Children's Books
A division of Hodder Headline Limited
338 Euston Road, London NW1 3BH

The right of Margaret Ryan to be identified as the author and
Bridget MacKeith the illustrator of this Work has been asserted
by them in accordance with the Copyright, Designs and Patents Act 1988.

Designed by Don Martin
Printed in Hong Kong by Wing King Tong

British Library Cataloguing in Publication Data available

ISBN 0 7500 2844 0

MARGARET RYAN

Robbie and the Alien

Illustrated by Bridget MacKeith

HODDER
Wayland

an imprint of Hodder Children's Books

Robbie liked school. He liked his
teacher, Miss Dobbs, and his friends,
Amelia and Ben. But today he didn't
want to go to school.

"I feel sick," he said at breakfast.
"You don't look sick," said his mum.
"You look nice in your new red jersey."

"You don't look sick," said his dad.
"You ate up lots of toast."
"You don't look sick," said his little
sister. "You look horrible."
"Go to school, Robbie," they all said.

But Robbie didn't want to go to school.
"I think it's a holiday today," he said.
"No, that was last week," said his mum.

"Or was it the week before?"
said his dad.

"I know why Robbie doesn't want
to go to school," said his little sister.
"It's because he's got to wear his new
glasses!"

Robbie made a face.

"The glasses are horrible," he said.

"Everyone will call me names."

"No, they won't," said his mum.

"I'm sure they won't," said his dad.

"Yes, they will," said his little sister.
"They'll call him **specky four-eyes!**"
But Robbie still had to go to school.

His mum made him put his new
glasses on when he left the house.
He still had them on at the garden gate.
He still had them on at the corner.
But as soon as he left his mum at the
corner he took them off.

That's when…
He fell over a cat and bumped his knee.

He fell over a dog and bumped his nose.

He walked into a wall and bumped his
head. Robbie rubbed the sore bits.

"I think I'd better put my new glasses back on," he said. The new glasses felt funny sitting on his nose. But he could see where he was going.

He went into the school playground
and met Amelia. Robbie waited for
Amelia to shout, "**Specky four-eyes!**"

But she didn't. Amelia had news.
"Miss Dobbs has a big surprise for us,"
she said. "She told me to tell everyone."

He went into the cloakroom and met
Ben. Robbie waited for Ben to shout,
"Specky four-eyes!"
But he didn't. Ben had news.

Have you heard?

"Miss Dobbs has a big surprise for us,"
Ben said. "She told me to tell everyone."
Robbie hurried into his classroom,
and saw the surprise.

She was sitting in his seat. She had
four hands, three legs and two heads.

"This is KT," said Miss Dobbs.
"She's an alien. I bumped into her
in the playground this morning.
Say hello to KT everyone."

20

"Hello, KT," said the class.

KT giggled and opened both mouths.

"Hello, everyone," she said.

"KT is very clever," said Miss Dobbs.
"I'm sure she can teach us lots of things.
Robbie, will you sit beside her?"

KT looked funny, but nice.

Robbie sat down next to her.

"Can I ask you something?" he said.

KT nodded both heads.

"Why have you got four hands?"
"To help me do things more quickly,"
said KT. "Wouldn't you like to have
an extra pair of hands sometimes?"

"Yes," said Robbie, "when I have
to tidy my bedroom. Can I ask you
something else?"
KT nodded both heads again.

"Why have you got three legs?"
"To help me run more quickly," said
KT. "Wouldn't you like to have three
legs sometimes?"

"Yes," said Robbie. "Then I could win
the three-legged race on sports day. Can
I ask you one last thing?"
KT nodded both heads once more.

"Why have you got two heads?"

"To help me think more quickly,"
said KT. "Haven't you heard that
two heads are better than one?
Now can I ask *you* something?"
Robbie nodded his one head.

"Why have you got little round glass things sitting on your nose?"

Robbie's face went red.
"To help me see better," he said.
"Without my glasses I fall over cats and dogs and walk into walls."

"I would like two pairs of glasses to
stop me bumping into things," said KT.
"That's how I met Miss Dobbs. She
didn't bump into me, I bumped into *her*."
Just then Miss Dobbs looked up from
her desk.

28

"You look different today, Robbie,"
she said.
Robbie's face went red again.
"Oh no," he whispered to KT.
Miss Dobbs is going to talk about
my new glasses. Then everyone will
call me **specky four-eyes!**"

"I know what's different," smiled
Miss Dobbs. "It's your new red jersey.
I'd love a jersey like that."
Robbie grinned. "I'll ask my gran
to knit you one," he said.

Have fun reading other BRIGHT STARS titles!

Robbie and the Pirate *by Margaret Ryan*
Robbie is scared of lots of things. He's scared of Growler the dog. He's scared of Tiger the cat. And most of all, he's scared of the Grump twins. But he's not scared of Blackbeard the pirate, who shows him how to stand up to everyone else!

Mulberry Alone on the Farm *by Sally Grindley*
Mulberry visits a farm for the day. He runs off to look for someone to play with, but the hens, the piglets and the scarecrow don't want to play with him. Mulberry is fed up, until the sky grows dark and he is caught in the middle of a scary thunderstorm...

Mulberry Alone at the Seaside *by Sally Grindley*
Mulberry has come to the seaside. He has great fun splashing in the sea and knocking down sand-castles. He even helps himself to someone's picnic. But when Mulberry is trapped by the tide, he decides he's had enough of the seaside for one day.

All these books and many more in the *Bright Stars* series can be purchased from your local bookseller. For more information, write to: *The Sales Department, Macdonald Young Books, 61 Western Road, Hove, East Sussex BN3 1JD.*